THIS CHRISTMAS BOOK
BELONGS TO

~~Sheila~~

~~Gerald~~

....

LADYBIRD BOOKS

UK | USA | Canada | Ireland | Australia | India | New Zealand | South Africa

Ladybird Books is part of the Penguin Random House group of companies
whose addresses can be found at global.penguinrandomhouse.com.

www.penguin.co.uk   www.puffin.co.uk   www.ladybird.co.uk

Penguin
Random House
UK

First published in Australia by Puffin Books 2020
This edition published in Great Britain by Ladybird Books Ltd 2022
004

Text and illustrations copyright © Ludo Studio Pty Ltd 2020

 BBC STUDIOS

Printed in China

The authorized representative in the EEA is Penguin Random House Ireland,
Morrison Chambers, 32 Nassau Street, Dublin D02 YH68

A CIP catalogue record for this book is available from the British Library

ISBN: 978-0-241-55199-8

All correspondence to:
Ladybird Books, Penguin Random House Children's
One Embassy Gardens, 8 Viaduct Gardens, London SW11 7BW

MIX
Paper | Supporting
responsible forestry
FSC **FSC® C018179**
www.fsc.org

BLUEY

CHRISTMAS EVE WITH
VERANDAH SANTA

It's Christmas Eve, and Bluey's whole family
has gathered at the Heeler house.

Everyone's already had dinner, which means
it's nearly time for Santa to come!

Bluey is bursting with excitement! She can't wait to open the presents that are already under the tree.

"*Uh-uh-uh.* No peeking at those presents," warns Dad.

"Why not?" asks Bluey.

"Because Santa doesn't give presents to naughty kids," says Dad.

Muffin wants to know how Santa gets in when there's no chimney.
"Maybe he uses the verandah," suggests Bluey.
Bingo bursts out from behind the presents.
"Let's play **Verandah Santa!**"

Muffin jumps off the chair and lands on her dad's belly.

"Muffin, quick, you have
to say sorry," says Bingo.
"Santa's watching!"
Bluey reminds her.

ARGHH!
I'M SORRY!

Now it's time to play the game! Bluey suggests Dad is Verandah Santa. The kids rush into bed and pretend to be asleep. "OK, it's Christmas in the morning. Remember, **no peeking** or **no presents!**" calls Dad as he walks out of the door.

HOORAY!

Dad **tiptoes** across the verandah and into the room. Bingo giggles with excitement, and Bluey opens one eye. "Was that a peek?" asks Dad.

Bluey shuts her eye
and shakes her head.
"It wasn't a peek!"

"Ho, ho and ho," says Dad
as he slips the presents
under the pillows.

It's morning! Verandah Santa has left something under everyone's pillow.
"Hooray!" cry the kids.

I GOT A SNOW GLOBE!

I GOT SHAVING CREAM!

I GOT A PENCIL CASE!

"Hey, that's my pencil case," yells Bingo, snatching it from Bluey.
"Yeah, but it's Bluey's for the game," says Dad. "She'll give
it back after."
Bingo apologizes, but Bluey doesn't want to accept her sorry.

"Why should I?" asks Bluey.
"Because Santa won't bring you
any presents!" explains Bingo.

SANTA LIKES CHILDREN
WHO ACCEPT SORRYS.

"OK, fine!" says Bluey
and takes the pencil case.

Now it's Bluey's turn to be Verandah Santa.
She grabs the hat and walks to the door.

NIGHT-NIGHT, KIDS.
NO PEEKING OR
NO PRESENTS.

"We won't!" they
chorus from the bed.

Bluey **tiptoes** across the verandah and into the room.
She reaches the bed and . . .

"Naughty children! You peeked at Santa," she says.
"No presents for you. I'm going to throw these in the bin!"
Bluey walks away, but the trio jump out of bed to protest.

Muffin, Bingo and Dad all put on their very best "please" faces.
"We're sorry, Santa," says Bingo.
"**Please** will you accept our sorry?" asks Dad.

"Hmmm." Bluey thinks for a moment, then decides she will.

"I sure am a very nice child!" says Bluey. "If I were the real Santa, I'd give me **lots** of presents!"

It's Bingo's turn now, and Socks rushes in to be her helper.
As Bingo goes to hand out the presents, Dad scoops her up . . .

OH, MY TEDDY BEAR.

RRRRUFF!

Bluey copies Dad and picks
up Socks. But Socks is
frightened and nips Bluey.

"Socks bit me!" yells Bluey.
Dad explains to Socks that it's not nice to bite people.
But that's not enough for Bluey.

"She's not even saying sorry!"
cries Bluey.
Dad shakes his head. "Socks is
only one and doesn't know any
better. Let's keep playing."

Bluey **tiptoes** across the verandah and into the room.
She creeps across the bed, avoiding grabby hands, to deliver
the presents. "HO, HO, HO and . . ."

Bluey yells, "Christmas!"
Everyone looks under their pillow for a present.

But there is nothing under Socks's pillow.

"Bluey!" says Dad as Socks runs out of the room.
"But she bit me and didn't say sorry!" huffs Bluey.

Afterwards, Mum and Dad find Bluey in the lounge room.
"Bluey, I think you should say sorry to Socks," says Dad.
"I was teaching her that Santa doesn't give you presents
if you're not nice," declares Bluey.

"That's not the reason to be nice to people," explains Mum.
"Then what *is* the reason?" asks Bluey.
Mum and Dad show Bluey that Socks is sitting outside on
her own, crying.

"Imagine if Socks did to you what you did to her," says Dad.
Bluey looks at Socks and thinks . . .

She realizes she would be sad, too. "Hi, Socks. I'm sorry I didn't give you any presents. I was mad because you didn't say sorry," says Bluey. Socks gives Bluey a lick, accepting the sorry in her own way.

There's time for one last game of Verandah Santa.

"OK, night, kids. Remember,
no peeking or no presents,"
says Dad as he goes to the door.

Dad **tiptoes** across the verandah and into the room.

HO, HO . . . OH NO!